For Deborah
~ D.B.
For Maddy
~ E.F.

LITTLE TIGER PRESS

An imprint of Magi Publications

1 The Coda Centre, 189 Munster Road, London SW6 6AW, UK

www.littletigerpress.com

First published in Great Britain 2000

First American edition published by Tiger Tales 2001

This edition published 2010

Text copyright © David Bedford 2000

Illustrations copyright © Elaine Field 2000

David Bedford and Elaine Field have asserted their rights

to be identified as the author and illustrator of this work

under the Copyright, Designs and Patents Act, 1988

All rights reserved • ISBN 978-1-84895-203-4

Printed in China • LTP/1800/0153/0910

2 4 6 8 10 9 7 5 3 1

LITTLE TIGER PRESS

It's my turn!

by David Bedford

illustrated by Elaine Field

Playground

Oscar and Tilly found a playground.
"Shall we play on the slide?" asked Oscar.
"I'll go first," said Tilly.

"I'll go now," said Oscar.
"Not yet," said Tilly.
"It's not your turn."

"That looks like fun," said Oscar. "Is it my turn now?" "Not yet," said Tilly.

Tilly went round and round on the merry-go-round.
"Is it my turn yet?" asked Oscar.
"No," said Tilly. "I haven't finished."

Tilly went round
and round
and round
and ROUND . . .

"I feel dizzy," said Tilly.

"Hee, hee," cried Oscar.
"It's my turn now,
you're too dizzy!"

"I feel better now," said Tilly.
"Can I slide after you?"
"No," said Oscar. "It's not your turn."

"Can I go on the swing after you?"
asked Tilly.
"No," said Oscar. "It's still my turn."

"Get off, Tilly," shouted Oscar.
"It's my turn on the see-saw."
"The see-saw doesn't work," said Tilly.
But when Oscar jumped on the other end . . .

Then Tilly
came down
and . . .

Oscar went up . . .

WHOO!

Oscar and Tilly
played together
all afternoon.